This igloo book belongs to:

........Charlie Ross G........

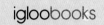

igloobooks

Published in 2019
by Igloo Books Ltd
Cottage Farm
Sywell
NN6 0BJ
www.igloobooks.com

0819 001.01
2 4 6 8 10 9 7 5 3 1
ISBN: 978-1-78905-672-3

Written by Melanie Joyce
Illustrated by Dubravka Kolanovic

Printed and manufactured in China

LITTLE LOST
PENGUIN

igloobooks

Here's an egg.
Sshh... listen.

It goes crack, crack, crack.
It tips this way and then rocks back.

A crack.

A snap.

A creak and a sneak of
a peek at a tiny little beak.

Then, a wing. A feather.
Both feet together.

Awoo goes the wind. It begins to blow and rocks the egg to and fro.

The egg slips and tips.

Out pops a little penguin. Then....

"...*"Grrrr*," goes a voice. It's a hairy bear.

"Who's there?" growls the bear.
Little Penguin is scared.

Little Penguin waddles to the sea.
Pitter-pitter-pat. A drop lands.

Splat,

splat,

splat!

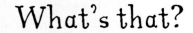

What's that?

There's a spout and a tail.
It's a whale.

SPLOSH!

Little Penguin gets a wash.

Plip-plop.

Drip-drop.

"I'm all wet," he says.

Then...

... from the sea comes a flipper, then a snout.
Something jumps out.

It's wriggly, jiggly, wibbly, wobbly.

"Urgh!" cries Little Penguin, running off to hide.

Little Penguin waddles
from side to side.

... roly-poly...

Slip-slide.

He skids and trips...

... *rumble-tumble...*

... FLUMP!

Then...

There's a nose and toes. An eye, then two.

"Who are you?" asks Little Penguin.
"I'm Fox," says the fox. Yap-snap.

In the sky, something flies.
It swoops and loops-the-loop.
Down it dives, clacking its beak. "Eeeek!"

"It's scary here," says Little Penguin,
running in fear.

Snow comes quick and thick.

It falls on his feathers, his nose, his tummy, his toes.

Little Penguin has an idea in his head.
"I know," he says.
"I'll go back to my egg."

So, back he goes and climbs inside.
"I'll be safe in here, where I can hide."

Everything is still and as dark as night.
Then, there's the tiniest little crack of light.

There's a wing. A feather. Two wings together.

There's a beak. An eye. Then another.
"Hello," says a voice. "I'm your mother."

Little Penguin is scooped into a pillowy hug,
like the softest cloud and he says out loud...

... "Mummy."

Mummy says, "We've all been looking for you.
Bear, Whale, Seal, Fox and Gull helped us, too."

"Thank you," said Little Penguin. At last he was home.
Never again would he be alone.

Happy Little Penguin

says, "Goodbye!"